THE BEAR
DETECTIVES

For Oliver and George Downward,
who listened to me telling stories
on October 13, 2008
S.G.

For Sam
J.B.

ORCHARD BOOKS
338 Euston Road, London NW1 3BH
Orchard Books Australia
Hachette Children's Books
Level 17/207 Kent Street, Sydney NSW 2000

First published in 2009
First paperback publication in 2010

Text © Sally Grindley 2009
Illustrations © Jo Brown 2009

A CIP catalogue record for this book is available from the British Library

ISBN 978 1 84616 155 1 (hardback)
ISBN 978 1 84616 163 6 (paperback)

1 3 5 7 9 10 8 6 4 2 (hardback)
1 3 5 7 9 10 8 6 4 2 (paperback)

Printed in China

Orchard Books is a division of Hachette Children's Books,
an Hachette UK company.

www.hachette.co.uk

The Mysterious Earth

Written by **SALLY GRINDLEY**
Illustrated by **JO BROWN**

ORCHARD BOOKS

Constable Tiggs

Sergeant Bumble

Postbear

One morning, Constable Tiggs
looked out of the police-house
window and saw something
brown on the village green.

He ran upstairs to tell Sergeant
Bumble.

"Wake up, Sergeant Bumble!"
he called. "There's something
brown on the village green."

"Eh? What sort of something?"
mumbled Bumble.

"I don't know," said Tiggs.

"Shall I go and investigate?"

"Wait for me," said Bumble. "That
something might be dangerous."

As soon as he was ready, they set off.

When they reached the green,
they tiptoed slowly towards
the something brown.

"What do you think it is?"
whispered Bumble.
"It looks like a pile of earth to me,"
said Tiggs.

"That's just what I was going to say," said Bumble. "This is serious. We can't have someone leaving piles of earth on our village green. We must have it removed."

Later that day, the postbear rushed into the police house and said, "You'll never believe it, Sergeant Bumble, but there's another pile of earth on the village green."

"What!" exploded Bumble. "Did
you see anyone putting it there?"
"Not a soul," said the postbear.
"One minute the green was all green,
the next there was more brown."

"This is serious," said Bumble.
"More serious than ever," said Tiggs.
"We'll have to keep watch to see
who is tipping earth on our green,"
said Bumble.

They went back to the green
and hid behind some bushes.
They waited and waited,
but nothing happened.

Bumble grew tired and sat down.
Soon his eyes began to close.
Tiggs watched some bears playing
catch and wished he could join in.

When the ball rolled in his direction, Tiggs jumped up to throw it back. As he did, he saw that another patch of brown had appeared on the green.

"Wake up, Sergeant
Bumble!" he cried.
"There's another one."
"Eh – what? Did
you see who it was?"
Bumble asked.

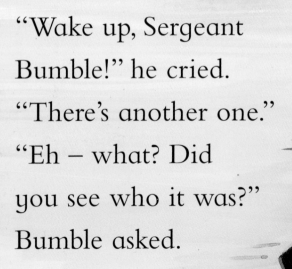

"There was nobody
here apart from those
bears playing catch,"
Tiggs replied.
"Are you sure you
didn't fall asleep?"
"I was awake all the
time, and I didn't see
anybody," said Tiggs.

"Well, this is a real mystery,"
said Bumble, scratching his head.
"Unless – perhaps it dropped from
the sky?"

They both looked up. The sky was empty for as far as they could see.

When they looked down again,
there was another small pile of
earth right next to their feet.
They couldn't believe it!

"Impossible!"
blustered
Bumble.

"I've had a thought," said Tiggs excitedly. "If the earth wasn't dropped *down* from the sky, perhaps it was pushed *up* from the ground."

"What on *earth* are you talking about, Constable Tiggs?" said Bumble.

"That pile of earth is growing, Sir."
They stood and watched. The pile
of earth grew bigger and bigger in
front of their very eyes.

"Well, bless my soul!" exclaimed
Bumble. "The earth is moving!"
Just then, a little black head poked
out through the top of the pile.
"Hello," it said.
Bumble and Tiggs stared
in astonishment.

"Why are you
digging up our
green?" asked Bumble.
"I'm a mole," said the head,
"and digging is what moles do."

"Not on our green, they don't,"
Bumble objected.
"Does that mean I've got to move?"
said the mole sadly.

Tiggs looked around. "Perhaps you could live in that lovely meadow over there?" he said.

The mole's face lit up. "That meadow does look nice! Can I come back and visit sometimes?"

"Of course you can," smiled Tiggs.

They watched as the mole skipped
around her new home.
Soon, she began to dig furiously.
A pile of earth appeared and grew
bigger and bigger...

"That's another mystery solved, then," said Bumble. "And now I think we deserve a nice cup of tea."

SALLY GRINDLEY ♣ JO BROWN

Bucket Rescue	978 1 84616 160 5
Who Shouted Boo?	978 1 84616 159 9
The Ghost Train	978 1 84616 161 2
Treasure Hunt	978 1 84616 158 2
The Mysterious Earth	978 1 84616 163 6
The Strange Pawprint	978 1 84616 164 3
The Missing Spaghetti	978 1 84616 165 0
A Very Important Day	978 1 84616 162 9

All priced at £4.99

Orchard Colour Crunchies are available from all good bookshops,
or can be ordered direct from the publisher:
Orchard Books, PO BOX 29, Douglas IM99 1BQ
Credit card orders please telephone 01624 836000
or fax 01624 837033 or visit our website: www.orchardbooks.co.uk
or e-mail: bookshop@enterprise.net for details.

To order please quote title, author and ISBN
and your full name and address.
Cheques and postal orders should be made payable to 'Bookpost plc.'
Postage and packing is FREE within the UK
(overseas customers should add £2.00 per book).

Prices and availability are subject to change.